P9-CNI-406
MESA PUBLIC LIBRARY
50814731

For Will and Justin

First edition 2011

Library of Congress Cataloging-in-Publication Data

Klassen, J.
I want my hat back / Jon Klassen. —1st ed.
p. cm.
Summary: A bear almost gives up his search for his missing hat until he remembers something important.
ISBN 978-0-7636-5598-3
[1. Bears—Fiction. 2. Hats—Fiction. 3. Lost and found possessions—Fiction.]
PZ7. K6781446Ih 2011
[E]—dc22 2010042793

17 18 19 20 APS 20 19

Printed in Humen, Dongguan, China

This book was typeset in New Century Schoolbook.
The illustrations were created digitally and in Chinese ink.

Candlewick Press
99 Dover Street
Somerville, Massachusetts 02144

visit us at www.candlewick.com

I WANT MY HAT BACK

JON KLASSEN

CANDLEWICK PRESS

My hat is gone.
I want it back.

Have you seen my hat?

No. I haven't seen your hat.

OK. Thank you anyway.

Have you seen my hat?

No. I have not seen any hats around here.

OK. Thank you anyway.

Have you seen my hat?

No. Why are you asking me.
I haven't seen it.
I haven't seen any hats anywhere.
I would not steal a hat.
Don't ask me any more questions.

OK. Thank you anyway.

Have you seen my hat?

I haven't seen anything all day. I have been trying to climb this rock.

Would you like me to lift you on top of it?

Yes, please.

Have you seen my hat?

I saw a hat once.
It was blue and round.

My hat doesn't look like that.
Thank you anyway.

Have you seen my hat?

What is a hat?

Thank you anyway.

Nobody has seen my hat.
What if I never see it again?
What if nobody ever finds it?

My poor hat.
I miss it so much.

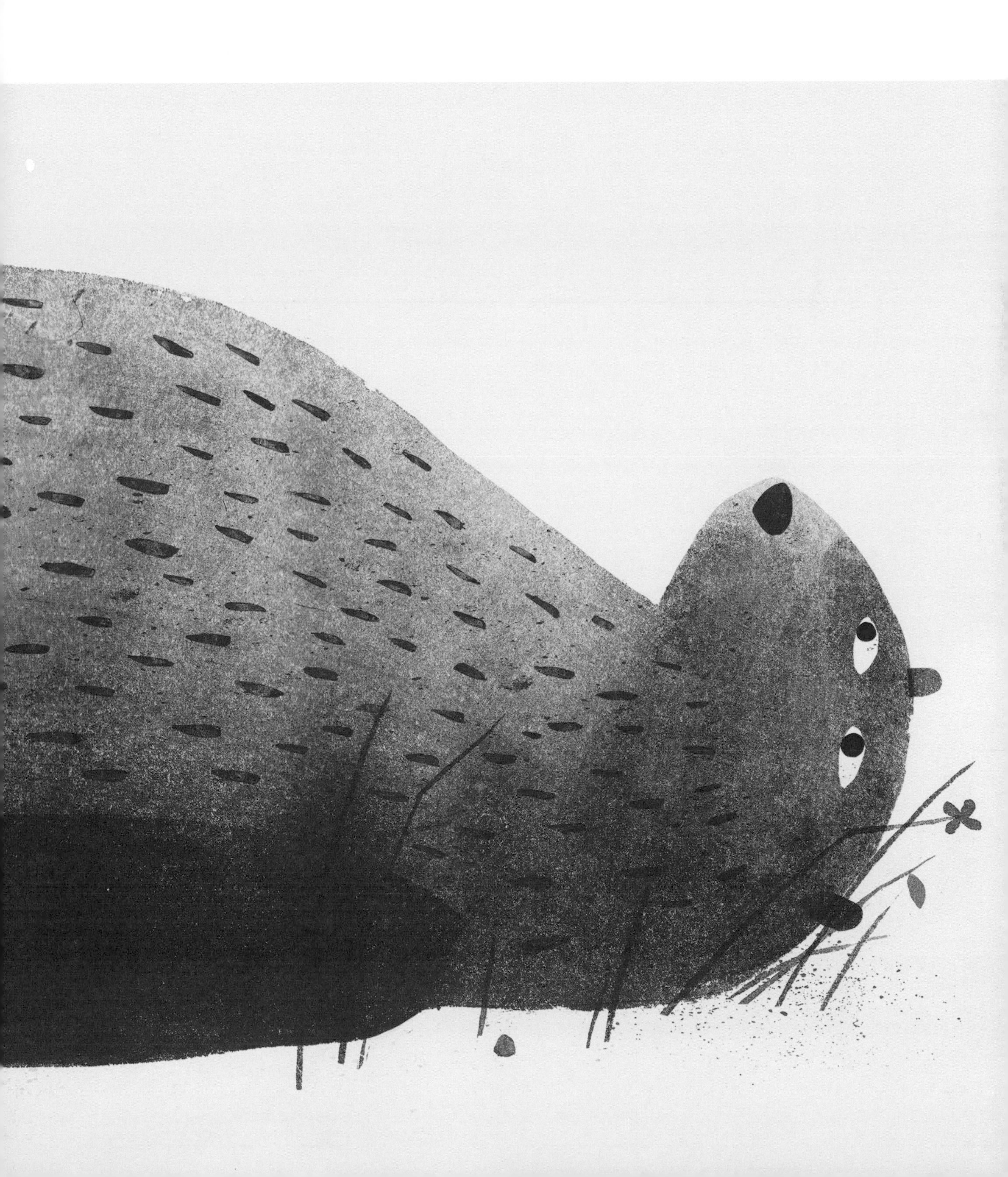

What's the matter?

I have lost my hat.
And nobody has seen it.

What does your hat look like?

It is red and pointy and . . .

I HAVE
SEEN MY HAT.

YOU. YOU STOLE MY HAT.

I love my hat.

Excuse me, have you seen
a rabbit wearing a hat?

No. Why are you asking me.
I haven't seen him.
I haven't seen any rabbits
anywhere.
I would not eat a rabbit.
Don't ask me any more questions.

OK. Thank you anyway.